THE APPLE AND THE INFINITE

JEREMY D SCHOLZ

For information or permission requests, please contact:

Jeremy D Scholz

https://jeremydscholz.com/

ISBN: 979-8-9994313-4-9

Printed in the United States of America

First Edition

The Apple and the Infinite

by Jeremy D Scholz

jeremydscholz.com

I dedicate this book to my colleague and friend, Rachel Nieman. One afternoon, as we prepared for the upcoming school year, she voiced a familiar frustration, the lack of engaging literature that connects young readers to the great figures of science. With her trademark blend of snark and professionalism, she quipped, "You should be useful and write one."

Though her comment was delivered half in jest, it carried the weight of a challenge. It sparked in me the realization that there truly is a need for stories that not only entertain but also inspire curiosity about the minds who shaped our understanding of the world. This book is, in many ways, an answer to that challenge.

So, to Rachel, thank you for your humor, your candor, and your ability to see both the gaps and the possibilities. Without your words, this story might never have been written.

J.S.

INTRODUCTION

The wind in Lincolnshire argues with everything. No one argues back. Not even the boy in the attic of Woolsthorpe Manor, the one who keeps a notebook the way other boys keep pocketknives.

His name is Isaac Newton, and he isn't supposed to be anybody remarkable.

He's supposed to be a farmer, count sheep, trade at market, nod at the minister. He's supposed to stop asking why smoke climbs and why the moon never falls. He's supposed to stop carving gears from willow wood and whispering questions to the dark.

But Isaac's life already knows the sound of breaking. His father died before he was born. His mother, remarried for security, and her new husband would not have another man's child in his house.

This is not a tale of a genius who wakes one morning and invents gravity from a falling apple. It's the story of a lonely, stubborn boy who notices what everyone else steps over.

Let's Begin –

"I do not know what I may appear to the world, but to myself I seem to have been only like a boy playing on the seashore, diverting myself... whilst the great ocean of truth lay all undiscovered before me."

~Isaac Newton~

1

———

QUIET BOY OF WOOLSTHORPE

Woolsthorpe-by-Colsterworth, Lincolnshire, *1659*

The wind came first. Before the snow, before the cold settled into the joints of the stone house, the wind howled across the rolling fields of Woolsthorpe Manor. Swirling air curled around chimneys and clawed at shutters like a living thing. It made the old oaks groan and the hens in the coop cluck in an uneasy rhythm.

Inside, a draft crept beneath the heavy oak door, sliding icy fingers along the stone floor and into the hem of young Isaac Newton's trousers. He didn't move. By now, he had long since learned how to ignore discomfort. His thin frame sat motionless in the corner of the great room, folded into itself like a collapsed easel. A faded wool blanket hung from his shoulders like a shawl, but his attention was fixed entirely on the open window before him, Sand on the tiny brass pendulum swinging in his hand.

Tick. Pause. Tick.

He was trying to match its rhythm to the tapping of a dripping leak in the corner. Water fell from the roof with surprising regularity, each drop falling from a beam overhead into a tin pan he had placed beneath it. At first, the leak had annoyed him, but now it fascinated him. He held the pendulum beside the pan, adjusting its length by fractions of an inch, trying to match each arc with a splash. When they finally synchronized, a quiet thrill rippled through his chest.

He jotted a note in the leather-bound book tucked beside him:

Regular drops = regular motion. Water, weight, time. Are all things ordered?

He stared at the words. Something about them stirred him, though he couldn't say why. Then the wind rattled the shutters again, louder this time, as if to remind him that the world didn't care for quiet epiphanies. Not out here, where the necessities of life demanded attention.

A clatter of metal in the adjoining kitchen made

him startle. He heard his grandmother's grumbling, her voice like gravel dragged across wood.

"Boy, did you stoke the fire yet, or are you still playing with ghosts and shadows?"

She doesn't understand, he thought.

Isaac slipped his notebook beneath the folds of his coat and stood slowly, his limbs stiff from sitting. He passed the wooden table cluttered with mechanical scraps, wooden gears, a makeshift pulley, pieces of glass, and a burned-out lantern that had once sparked with blue fire before extinguishing itself with a hiss. That project had failed, but he had documented every step in his journal. Failure, he had decided, was only a name for information not yet understood.

At the hearth, he prodded the logs until orange sparks flew upward like tiny comets, swirling briefly before vanishing. He loved watching fire. It didn't just burn; it danced. It flickered with patterns, like thoughts turned into motion.

He didn't speak unless spoken to. He had learned this years ago, when his questions: Why does smoke rise? Why does the sun set slower in summer? had earned him cuffs to the ear or sharp rebukes from adults too tired to answer. So, he asked in silence. To himself. To notebooks. To the world, which he watched with endless curiosity.

The fire caught and warmed the room. The smell of old ash mixed with wood resin and a faint tang of coal. His grandmother grunted in approval from the kitchen.

He let the warmth settle over his hands, then turned to survey the day's light. Outside, the fields were colorless, bare soil, faded grass, the skeletal branches of apple trees scratching at the gray sky. From this window, he could just see the stables, where his small weather vane spun wildly on its wooden post. He had built it from an old butter churn, a knife blade, and the tail of a broken kite. It worked, crudely but truthfully. He smiled to himself in quiet satisfaction.

Isaac's room was in the attic. It had once been his father's room, before death had claimed him.

Isaac had never known his father. He had died just months before Isaac was born, a farmer with strong hands and a proud brow. The manor, the land, and the animals had all belonged to the elder Isaac Newton, and now they were passed down to a boy too young to carry a spade, let alone a legacy.

His mother, Hannah, had grieved. For a while.

But grief turned to practicality, and practicality turned to marriage. A wealthy clergyman offered her security, stability, and a life away from the hardships of managing a farm alone. He had one condition: the boy could not come.

So Isaac stayed behind.

At the age of three, he was left at Woolsthorpe in the care of his grandmother. His mother moved to another village with her new husband and began a new life, one in which her firstborn had no place.

He remembered very little of her now. Her voice was a faint echo. Her face, a blur. Her absence, however, was clear, like a stain that would not wash out.

The stairs creaked as he climbed, careful not to let the nail heads catch his stockings. The attic door stuck slightly, too.

It was the water. It was too damp here.

He forced the door open and ducked into his room, his sanctuary.

The room was cold but alive with activity. Diagrams were pinned to the slanted walls, glass jars held dusted minerals and dried herbs, and a clock lay in stages of disassembly on a side table. Candles sat in various states of waxy decay. A cracked window let in both light and cold air, but he didn't mind.

On the desk lay his windmill, a masterpiece of boyish ingenuity. The blades were cut from willow wood and sanded until smooth. The axle spun on a hand-whittled dowel, suspended in tiny carved cradles. It had worked once. The wind had caught it and turned it, only briefly, before a sudden gust had knocked it from the sill and shattered one of its legs. He had retrieved the pieces and set them here, intending to repair it.

He picked up the base and turned it in his hands. The splintered wood scratched at his fingertips, and he examined the crack the way a surgeon might examine a wound. His mind filled with possibilities, reinforcement, counterweight, improved balance. He made a note on a scrap of parchment:

Add cross-brace to stabilize lower shaft. Test in 2 days.

A scratching at the window startled him. Just a bare apple branch, twisted by wind, tapping at the glass. He let out a breath he had been holding.

The orchard outside looked dead now, but in summer it burst with fruit, fat, sweet apples that fell and bruised when he didn't get to them in time. Once, he had watched one fall. It hadn't been dramatic. It had just... let go. Dropped. A clean arc from branch to earth. But something about that arc stayed with him. Not the falling, everything fell, but the sameness of it. Whether it was an apple, a stone, or a clump of snow from the rooftop, things dropped down. Always. Why?

He picked a dried apple from a bowl by his bed and held it in front of him, then let it fall.

Thump.

Again.

Thump.

He listened. Not to the sound, but to the motion.

Was the Earth pulling it? Was something else? Could the force that pulled the apple be the same one that kept the moon circling above the Earth, night after night?

He recorded a new thought:

"If a force acts on apples... perhaps it acts on the moon."

He stared at the sentence, blood humming behind his ears. That was a dangerous thought. Not blasphemous, not exactly, but bold. Too bold for a boy in his station.

The world had already decided who he was: the farmer's son. Abandoned, quiet, clever in inconvenient ways. He was meant to manage the land, tend the flocks, marry a local girl, and vanish into obscurity.

But his mind refused that fate.

He wasn't a farmer. There was nothing wrong with being a farmer, but farmers didn't lie awake at night wondering how time flowed or why things fell.

He moved to a small table in the corner where his

mechanical cart sat, a block of wood on four wheels, with a mouse cage tied to the back. The mice were long gone, escaped, but he still remembered how they had scurried forward when frightened, dragging the tiny cart in short bursts. He had tried to measure the force of their motion with sand timers. It hadn't worked precisely, but it had worked.

He had also built a water clock, using two jars and a pinprick hole to control the flow. The ink lines he had marked for each minute had bled in the damp, making them useless, but again, he had seen that time could be measured. That things happened in intervals, in sequence. It was there, under the surface of the world, like music only he could hear.

The wind howled again, this time accompanied by a flurry of snow. It scattered sideways across the orchard and slammed into the panes with a hiss of sleet. Isaac closed the window and turned back to the hearth. The flame was beginning to die. He added a log.

As the fire crackled, his grandmother called again, more softly this time.

"Come eat, boy."

He descended the stairs with his usual quiet, the shadows stretching around him like arms. The kitchen smelled of broth and root vegetables. That meant a pot of weak stew sat on the table. He sat down without a word. She handed him a bowl and tore him a piece of bread.

"You still tinkering with that wind toy?" Grandma inquired.

"Yes," he said simply. He knew where this was headed.

"You'll wear your eyes out looking at gears and paper."

"Maybe," he murmured, and sipped the stew.

Outside, snow blanketed the orchard, covering the paths, hiding the scars of the fallen apples, and muffling the wind. Inside, Isaac Newton sat by the fire, his hands wrapped around a warm bowl, and thought of mice, of water clocks, of the moon, and of apples.

The world, he decided, was filled with questions.

And if no one would, or more likely could, answer them for him, he would have to answer them himself.

2

THE APOTHECARY'S ATTIC

rantham, Lincolnshire, 1660

The road to Grantham ran east through the low fields, winding like a thread through stitched linen. In spring, it was a narrow, muddy track, flanked by sodden meadows and skeletal trees. Isaac sat atop the back of a cart filled with sacks of oats, his legs dangling over the edge, boots still caked with mud from the manor yard.

He didn't speak as the cart rocked over stones and potholes. His satchel rested firmly in his grip. Inside were two notebooks, his sketch of a water clock, a disassembled compass, and the remnants of his apple-drop experiments. He had wanted to bring more, but his grandmother had said, "It's not a laboratory, Isaac. You're going to school, not to the moon."

School. A place where boys laughed too loud and cared too little.

The driver, a leathery-faced man named Thomas West, chewed on a piece of straw and glanced over his shoulder. "You don't talk much, do you?"

"No," Isaac replied.

"Fair enough. Most talk my ear off, I don't mind the quiet," he said, keeping his eyes on the road as he held the reins.

They fell into silence, broken only by the steady rhythm of the wheels.

Grantham revealed itself slowly, first a church spire, then rooftops jutting like crooked teeth above the hedgerows. As they entered town, the air thickened with smoke and the mingled scents of manure, coal, and roasting meats. People passed on foot or horseback, shouting greetings, calling for hens, dragging sacks of barley through the muck.

Isaac kept his gaze low. He didn't like cities, even small ones like this. They were noisy, cluttered with chaotic human motion he could never diagram.

The cart stopped in front of William Clarke's apothecary shop, a narrow stone building with a painted sign of a mortar and pestle swinging above the door. A red fox pelt was nailed to the lintel, and dried herbs hung from the eaves. This would be Isaac's lodging.

He climbed down from the cart and stepped onto the cobbled street, the ground shifting strangely beneath his feet. Clarke greeted him with a thin-lipped smile and eyes that looked as if they had weighed a thousand herbs and found most of them wanting.

"You're the Newton boy, then? Quiet one. Come in."

The apothecary's home smelled of vinegar, lavender, and burnt sugar. Bottles lined the walls, green and brown glass filled with murky liquids, powders, and seeds. A one-eyed cat blinked at Isaac from the stair rail. He smiled at the order of the bottles, already wondering about the system used to arrange them.

He was given a room in the attic. It was narrow, with a sloped ceiling, a single dormer window, and a wooden cot. It was perfect.

Here, he could think. Here, no one would bother him.

Later that night, after a bland supper of stewed meat and vegetables, Isaac unpacked his satchel and arranged his few belongings with care: notebook on the desk, water clock parts on the sill, compass on the floor beside the bed. He opened the window to feel the night air, cooler here, with a faint metallic tang. From the spire down the hill, church bells tolled.

He couldn't sleep. Too many new angles, too many unfamiliar sounds. Rising in the dark, he began to draw, sketching the layout of the apothecary shop below: estimating the lengths of hallways, the incline of the staircase, the number of seconds between creaks in the floorboards as Clarke passed beneath him.

In the margin, he added a note: *Sleep evades precision.*

Isaac arrived at The King's School the next morning in a borrowed coat too large for him and shoes still slightly damp from the walk. The building itself was imposing, with high-arched windows, sandstone walls, and a courtyard echoing with the chatter of boys already well acquainted with one another.

He was an outsider.

A bell rang, summoning them inside. The boys hurried through the doors.

The classroom was dim and drafty, its wooden desks worn smooth by generations of elbows and quills. On the far wall, a Latin verse from Proverbs was painted in flaking gold: *Sapientia est potentia, Knowledge is power.* Francis Bacon had coined the phrase, and Isaac already believed it. It made him feel faintly as though he were in the right place.

Their schoolmaster, Mr. Stokes, was wiry, stern, and fond of recitations. He wore a wool robe that dragged across the floor like the hem of a ghost. When he pointed, it was always with two fingers, as though delivering a sermon, or lunging with a sword.

Isaac sat in the back at first. He listened. He didn't want attention, not yet. He took it all in, the desks, his fellow students, the scent of ink and chalk.

The other boys noticed him within minutes.

"Who's the crow in the corner?" one whispered.

"Farm boy," another snorted. "Smells of manure."

The boys laughed. Not particularly cruel, just boys filling their boredom with any new or different thing. Still, it wasn't kind. Isaac felt himself shrink from the attention.

It was Arthur Storer, broad-chested, loud, the son of a local merchant, who locked eyes with Isaac during their first geometry lesson and saw a threat. Arthur's answers were always quick, though not always correct.

When Isaac raised his hand, timidly at first, Mr. Stokes arched an eyebrow.

"Newton?"

Isaac answered with quiet precision.

Arthur's glare was immediate; his disapproval unmistakable. He did not like being bested by someone he considered a poor, dim farm boy. Arthur was used to being the smartest in the room.

The rivalry was born.

Clarke the apothecary was not an affectionate man, but he was a meticulous one, and Isaac respected that. In the evenings, Clarke allowed him to assist in the shop: grinding herbs, weighing powders, arranging tinctures in exact order of potency and use.

Isaac found this work meditative. He measured, categorized, and compared. Before long, he began keeping a second notebook, this one devoted to botanicals, reaction temperatures, and chemical stains.

One evening, Clarke found him boiling vinegar and chalk over the fire. The smell was foul.

"What in God's name are you doing?"

"Testing solubility. If I separate the acid..."

"You'll separate your eyebrows from your face if you're not careful," the older man said.

But he did not stop him, not completely. He gave him a burned alembic to tinker with, and Isaac nearly wept with gratitude. He continued to ask questions and test for answers. Francis Bacon would have approved.

It was during a lull in early March that the infamous skylight incident occurred.

Isaac had been studying prisms, so he had fashioned one from cut glass and sealed it in resin. He noticed how light shifted and bent through it, forming strange rainbows. *He wondered if light could be split. Could it be changed?*

So, he took a mirror from Clarke's storage and angled it to catch the early morning sun through the attic window. Then he placed the prism in front of it and watched as the beam splintered into color on the wall.

Red.

Orange.

Yellow.

Green.

Blue.

Indigo.

Violet.

He held his breath. He had made a discovery, yet it only raised more questions.

Were the colors always the same?

Did they always appear in the same order?

Why did bending light break it apart?

He repositioned the prism. The colors shifted.

He shaded the top half with parchment, and only the bottom half of the spectrum remained.

"Light has parts," he wrote. "It is not whole."

He built a second prism and, through it, recombined the colors into white light again.

A miracle, he thought.

Later that week, Clarke noticed the scorch mark on the attic floor and the cracked mirror. He said nothing, but the next day Isaac found an unused candlestick placed near the window. Though unspoken, it was clear Mr. Clarke was encouraging him. It was nice to have his investigations not merely tolerated but quietly supported.

3

ELIZA CLARKE

Clarke had a niece, Eliza Clarke. She was fifteen, sharp-eyed, freckled, and almost pathologically curious. She visited once a week to help in the shop, though she spent more time rearranging bottles in a chaotic version of alphabetical order and asking questions that Isaac both admired and found impossible to answer.

"Why do you always look like you're talking to ghosts?" she asked one afternoon.

"I don't," Isaac replied without looking up.

"You do. You stare at the air like it owes you something."

"Maybe it does," he said in his defense.

That made her laugh, a bright, sharp sound that

seemed too loud for the small room. He liked the sound of her laughter. She liked having someone closer to her age to talk to.

She never mocked his notebooks. In fact, she admired his organized thoughts. Once, she even asked to read one. He was tempted; he even wanted to, but experience had taught him to keep them private. Still, he allowed her to see his drawing of the redesigned windmill.

She leaned over the page, studying the fine details and the neat notes in the margins.

"Your mind must run faster than others," she said. "Furious and brilliant."

He blushed, pretending to write, though a quiet smile tugged at the corner of his mouth.

By late spring, Arthur Storer's pride had grown sore from Isaac's quiet, relentless correctness. He hated that Isaac was never wrong. Soon, he began challenging him openly in class.

"Newton, if you're so clever, solve this," he said one day, slapping a complex arithmetic problem onto the board. It was one he had pulled from one of the schoolmaster's books.

Isaac walked to the front without a word. He studied the problem, adjusted a single number, and solved it twice, first in figures, then in Latin prose.

Mr. Stokes raised an eyebrow. "Correct. Concise. Impressive. How did you do that?"

Arthur's cheeks burned red.

That night, Isaac found a note wedged under his desk.

Stay in your place, crow.

He didn't respond. What would he even say? Instead, he opened one of his private notebooks and penned a new equation: *Resistance ≠ correctness.*

In April, a storm unlike any he had ever seen swept through Grantham. Rain pounded the rooftops like fists, and the apothecary windows rattled in their frames. Thunder cracked like cannon fire, and instead of hiding, Isaac sat by the attic window, counting the seconds between each flash and boom.

He scribbled on parchment, calculating the distance of each strike by the time delay. The candle beside him flickered and danced in sync with the lightning.

It was beautiful.

He was no longer afraid of storms.

He would rather study them.

Isaac lay awake that night, the air still carrying the faint tang of ozone, thunder murmuring far off in the distance. In his hand, he held a piece of twine tied to a lead weight, his new pendulum prototype. In his mind, ideas swirled like clouds before a downpour.

For the first time, he felt something take shape beneath the surface of his thoughts, a system, a framework, a harmony. He didn't yet have the words for it, but he knew he would.

By late summer, the sun hung low behind the rooftops of Grantham, casting long golden shadows across the cobbled streets. The bustle of the day had faded, replaced by the quiet hum of evening. Inside the apothecary, the clinking of glass and the rustle of parchment had stilled. The shop was closed, the shutters drawn.

Outside on the worn stone steps, Isaac sat hunched with his knees drawn up, his fingers loosely wrapped around the edges of his sleeves.

Eliza stepped out from the doorway, brushing flour from her apron, and settled beside him without a word. For a while, they sat together in the hush of early evening, the only sounds the soft chirr of crickets and the distant clop of hooves.

"You're quiet," she said at last.

Isaac kept his gaze forward. "There was a fight today."

Eliza turned toward him, surprised. "You?"

He nodded slowly. "I didn't want to. I really didn't.

But the other boy... he kept shoving me. Laughing. He took my book and threw it in the mud."

Her brow furrowed. "So what did you do?"

"I told him to stop. He didn't. So, I hit him. Hard. We fought. I think I surprised him."

Eliza gave a low whistle, not mockingly. "Did you win?"

Isaac gave a half-shrug. "I don't know. It wasn't like that. It just... happened. I didn't want to be in it, but I felt like if I didn't fight back, I'd always be... smaller."

He paused, staring at his scuffed boots. "I don't know what it'll be like at school now. I didn't like how it felt."

Eliza was quiet for a moment. "I think you did what you had to do. But that doesn't mean it has to be who you are."

He looked up, his expression uncertain. She smiled gently.

"You're not like the others, Isaac. And that's not a bad thing."

A softer silence settled between them. Isaac exhaled and leaned back slightly, his shoulders loosening just a bit.

"I'd rather think," he said after a pause. "I'd rather understand how things work, why the stars move, why light bends, why time feels fast when you're dreaming. I think about those things. Not fists."

Eliza tilted her head, curious. "Why does light bend?"

His eyes brightened, just for a moment. "Well... I think it's because light isn't just one thing. When it passes through glass, like the curved lens of Mr. Clarke's magnifier, it splits, like it's made of many colors all traveling together."

"You've seen that?"

He nodded. "With a prism. It makes a rainbow."

"A rainbow in glass," she said, wonder threading through her voice.

He glanced at her, unsure if she was humoring him, but her eyes were earnest. He went on.

"And I think if you could find the rules for how it bends, you could find the rules for everything. Maybe even time. Maybe even the force that pulls everything toward the ground."

Eliza gave a small laugh, not mocking but rich with quiet delight. "You think like a storm in a bottle, Isaac Newton."

He smiled, almost surprised at himself.

They lingered there a while longer as the street grew dim. A breeze stirred the leaves across the cobblestones. The silence between them felt easy now, like a thought waiting patiently to be spoken.

"You'll be alright," Eliza said softly, standing and brushing off her apron. "Just don't stop thinking."

Isaac watched her go, then leaned back against the wooden doorframe, his eyes on the deepening sky.

For the first time that day, he didn't feel small.

4

___

BETWEEN FARM AND FORMULA

oolsthorpe-by-Colsterworth, Summer 1661
The sun pressed down with an oppressive weight, not sharp or punishing, but thick, like the closing words of a sermon stretched past its welcome. The air shimmered faintly above the fields, and the hum of flies filled the silence between the clank of harness and the groan of wood. Isaac Newton trudged behind the ox as the harrow dragged jagged teeth through the unyielding soil. Dust clouded his vision, mingling with the sweat that ran into his eyes and stung like salt on an open wound.

He squinted against the glare. His hands, raw from days of labor, gripped the reins out of duty rather than mastery. The beast hardly needed direction; it knew the path as well as Isaac did by now. Forward. Drag. Turn. Reset.

A rhythm, but not a song. More of a dirge.

He had been home for six weeks. Six weeks since the letter had arrived at Clarke's shop in Grantham, written in his mother's sharp, efficient hand.

"Isaac is to return home immediately. The farm needs tending. We expect him within a week."

No soft words.

No inquiry.

Only expectation, like an attractive force itself, inevitable and pulling. Isaac had not even known his mother was back at the farm.

Mr. Clarke read the letter silently, then handed it back without comment. Eliza, who had been arranging dried herbs near the window, went still. She had grown accustomed to Isaac's company, and now she would have to return to entertaining herself around the shop.

The next morning, Eliza pressed a tin of charcoal pencils into his hand, along with folded parchment.

"For diagrams," she said. Her eyes didn't meet his, but they shimmered.

He had walked most of the way to Woolsthorpe. The road felt longer than it had in winter, when he first came to Grantham, back when the world seemed wider. Now the dusty ruts wound back into the narrow valley of his birth, where fields rolled in dull repetition and the sky rarely seemed to move.

His mother did not look up when he arrived. The scent of baking bread and chicken clung to the air as she kneaded dough at the table.

"About time," she said. "You'll take over the lower field. Your uncle's taken ill. We need you here."

That was all. No welcome. No curiosity about his studies. No space for protest. Her new husband had died, and she had moved back to the farm with Isaac's step-siblings.

Now, dragging the harrow under the burning sun, Isaac muttered under his breath. Latin mostly, phrases from Ovid or Horace jumbled with his own equations. He tried to distract himself. He tried not to hate her. He did not mind hating the work.

Two crows watched from a hedge, their heads cocked like disapproving scholars.

"Clever birds," he whispered. "Go on, then. Fly."

They did not.

Labor improbus omnia vincit, Eliza had once scrawled in the margin of his book. *Hard work conquers all.*

He disagreed. Hard work battered the flesh. Ideas, though, they lived in silence, in stillness, in wonder.

Above, a cloud meandered across the sky, its shadow rippling over the field like a ghost. Isaac raised his thumb, tracking its course, calculating angles instinctively. A mental note: velocity relative to wind direction, rate of drift. He would sketch it later if there was still candlelight to spare.

"Isaac!" His mother's voice rang out like a thrown stone.

She stood at the barn's threshold, apron dusted with flour, arms folded like a stone gate.

"You're daydreaming again. The north plot isn't going to till itself."

His jaw tightened. He clicked his tongue, urging the ox forward.

That night, when the house had surrendered to sleep, Isaac crept to his room and eased up a creaking floorboard. Beneath it, wrapped in linen to keep off the mice, lay his true work, his notebook. The candle was nearly spent, but he lit the stub anyway, shielding it with cupped hands as though protecting a secret fire.

He opened the book. Pages buckled with humidity, corners curled, ink faded, yet the diagrams still whispered. Arcs traced in charcoal. Notes on sun declination. Observations of the orchard.

He picked up his quill.

Observed: *same branch, same time each day, apple falls. Always the same curve.*

He drew a line. Then another. Time intervals, curved vectors, possible wind resistance.

If resistance slows motion... what resists the moon? He stared at the question, then circled it twice.

The next morning, while hauling feed to the chickens, his mother blocked his path.

"You've your father's mind," she said, arms crossed. "And his folly."

Isaac blinked. She rarely spoke of his father.

"He left me with land, a child, and a roof barely holding. Wrote poetry about stars while the roof leaked. Do you understand?"

He nodded, lips pressed tight. He understood the words, but not what she truly meant.

"You're not in school anymore. That's done. You're needed here."

He didn't answer. That night, he scribbled in his notebook:

She sees poetry as failure. But what if poetry and force come from the same source?

By the third week, the barn had become his haven.

Two barrels and a plank served as his desk. From a cracked beam, he strung a pendulum weighted with a scrap of iron. A drip of wax marked each swing. He listened. Measured. Calculated.

Time it seemed, cared nothing for the pendulum's arc. Whether wide or narrow, the beat remained constant.

His heart leaped, another discovery.

Period of pendulum = constant. Arc and mass irrelevant.

He scrawled the formula. The candle hissed low. Overhead, the barn owl blinked.

This, this was motion. Not the trudge of an ox. Not toil. But discovery.

By late July, the orchard's early windfall began. Each afternoon, apples thudded softly onto the grass.

Isaac sat beneath the largest tree, its bark warm against his back. A green apple rested in his palm, half-eaten. He tossed it up and caught it. Again.

One dropped nearby. He watched it fall, not fast, not dramatic, but steady. Predictable.

Always down.

"Moon," he whispered, eyes lifting. "The moon... does it fall?"

He imagined flinging a stone from the tower in Grantham. Farther. Faster. What if one day it never came down?

What if it circled forever?

Curved fall. Infinite fall. Orbit.

His hand trembled as he opened the notebook. He pressed the quill to paper, ink smudging the edge of a thought too vast to name: *The force that pulls the apple... is not limited to Earth.*

One afternoon, while marking solar angles in chalk along the barn wall, Isaac heard hoofbeats. A rider approached, kicking up dust along the lane.

It was Reverend Babington.

The vicar dismounted slowly, peering at the markings with a mixture of confusion and amusement.

"You haven't changed," he said.

Isaac flushed. "It's just measurements."

"Just?" The Reverend chuckled. "You've drawn an ephemeris in your barn."

He stepped closer. "Have you thought of returning to school?"

Isaac hesitated. "I was at King's School. Before."

"And now?"

He looked away. "My mother needs me here."

Babington was quiet for a long moment.

"Would you like me to speak with her?"

Isaac stared down at the dirt, heart pounding. Then he nodded. Yes, more than anything, he thought.

He simply said, "Yes."

It took weeks. Quiet arguments. Tight-lipped meals.

In the end, it was the barley that changed her mind.

The crops failed. The north plot withered. The soil cracked.

His calculations, sun angles, shade intervals, irrigation paths, were no longer dismissed. They were studied.

"Go then," she said at last, not looking at him. "But don't waste it."

Isaac packed that night. His satchel strained not with clothes but with knowledge, pages upon pages, ideas still half-born.

He walked to the orchard, feeling freed from the farm yet grateful for the lessons learned there. The apple tree swayed slightly in the warm wind. He placed a hand on its bark, the texture rough beneath his calloused fingers.

"Thank you," he whispered, his voice reverent.

The stars spun silently above. Still distant, but no longer unreachable.

5

THE EYES OF CAMBRIDGE

O*ctober 1661—Trinity College, University of Cambridge*

The rain fell in a fine, persistent mist, soft as breath yet cold enough to slip through the seams of his coat. Isaac stood in the middle of the Great Court, boots sodden from the long walk, his breath blooming before him like steam from a kettle. Towering buildings flanked him, Trinity's limestone guardians, carved and weathered, their faces streaked with centuries of wind and memory. Water pooled between the cobbles, and the bells of Great St. Mary's had only just ceased their mournful tolling. The sound lingered in the back of his mind, like a hymn or a herald.

He gripped the leather strap of his satchel as if it

might anchor him, as if it might prove he belonged here. The bag was battered and nearly empty, holding only a crust of bread wrapped in linen, a flask of ink, two quills, and the most precious thing he owned: his notebooks. The pages were thick with diagrams and scattered Latin phrases, fragments of geometry, maps of the sky, and questions that had kept him awake long into the Woolsthorpe nights.

He had made it. Here, he hoped to find peers, equals.

And yet he felt like a trespasser among kings. Students flowed around him, their robes brushing his own like birds in migration. They moved in tight circles, boots polished, cloaks heavy with rich dye, Latin flowing easily, laughter looser still. Isaac caught fragments of their conversations.

"Descartes is a fool. Barrow dispatched him with two lines."

"Two lines too many. Have you seen the pudding tonight?"

Snorts of laughter. Cloaks flapping like wings.

One passed close and gave Isaac a second glance, not unkind, merely curious, but his eyes did not linger.

Isaac lowered his gaze and stepped aside. He could smell the damp wool of their garments, the faint trace of soap in their hair, and the smoke of early fires from the hall. They belonged. They were the sons of landowners, doctors, and magistrates. He was the son of a yeoman widow, a sizar come to earn his keep.

You are here to learn, he reminded himself. Not to belong.

His assigned quarters sat atop the building in Nevile's Court, reached by a narrow stairwell and through a door that groaned in protest each time he opened it. The room was barely the size of a cupboard, tucked beneath a slanted roof beam that kissed the top of his head if he stood too quickly.

The air smelled of old straw and damp timber. The mattress sagged in the middle. The hearth was lifeless.

But the desk—oh, the desk—faced east. At sunrise, light spilled across it in golden silence. Finally, a desk worthy of his notes.

He unpacked like a man preparing for a sacred ritual. He placed his notebook flat in the center, then set down his compass, his folding quadrant, and the half-used stub of a tallow candle. Each object was arranged with care, like relics, artifacts of his struggle to understand. His coat, still damp, hung from the crooked nail in the corner.

Then he sat, spine straight, hands flat on the desk. Beyond the warped glass of the garret window, the morning fog turned the chapel roof into a ghostly silhouette.

He whispered aloud, "Let's begin."

The university pressed against him, not with violence but with slow suffocation.

Corridors were thick with the ghosts of Milton and Erasmus, recitations rattling off like sermons. Rooms were heavy with chalk dust and the scent of pipe smoke. Every corner of Trinity spoke in a voice not its own—a lineage of men quoting other men, as though the act of speaking their names conferred truth.

Isaac listened. Always listened. He did not challenge aloud, not yet. But inside, friction sparked. Understanding could not simply be passed down like an inheritance. The learner must strive to understand.

He scratched notes furiously during lectures. Not only equations or translations but questions. He began compiling a ledger of wrong assumptions, statements made by revered philosophers that had no proof, only prestige.

"The Earth is the center."

"Motion requires constant force."

"The heavens are immutable."

In his garret, by moonlight and candle flame, he tore those certainties apart.

"What if motion was the natural state?"

"What if force created not chaos but law?"

"What if the heavens followed the same rules as apples falling from trees?"

The idea took root like frost across glass, quiet, relentless, and coldly beautiful.

He scrubbed pews in the chapel before sunrise. He polished boots that cost more than his entire tuition. He fetched firewood, cleaned chamber pots, and served at the high tables in the dining hall. He had to earn his way; no one was paying his way.

Some students looked past him. A few smirked. One or two offered him awkward kindnesses: half a loaf of bread, a nod in passing.

Isaac accepted nothing but silence; he earned his own way. He lived in his own world, a strange and ordered cosmos of thought and observation. He spoke not to fellow students but to the stars, to the geometry of water dripping from an eave, to the candle's flicker and the arc of shadows across stone walls.

When others gathered in alehouses or argued in the yard, he sat by his desk, transcribing Euclid by hand. He read Descartes in Latin and then read it again in English. He did not worship the ancients; he questioned them.

"They assume too much," he wrote in the margin of Aristotle. "Let nothing be assumed. Begin at zero."

A November storm rattled Cambridge to its bones. Rain swept in horizontal sheets across the courtyards. Thunder rolled low, like some sleeping God turning in the dark.

Isaac waited until the porters were abed. With his cloak pulled tight and a waxed sheet tucked over his notebooks, he slipped from his garret into the wet night. His feet squelched through puddles. The Wren Library loomed like a fortress, its doors barred and its lanterns unlit.

But Isaac knew the way in. He was not going to be denied the opportunity to learn.

There was a loose window at the rear, just large enough to crawl through. He had discovered it in his first week.

Inside, silence reigned like in a cathedral. He lit his candle and moved among the shelves, eyes scanning the spines. His hand hovered near the G's.

Galileo.

The name had flitted through the mouths of older students like a heresy.

"Obsessed with falling objects," one had sneered.

Madness, Isaac thought, might only be clarity out of season. Ideas should be tested and challenged, not feared and hidden.

He found the book. Fingers trembling, he turned the first page. The candle flickered. And he read. He read into the night and on through to the morning.

The next morning, sleepless and haggard, Isaac stood before Isaac Barrow. The Lucasian Chair of Mathematics was a narrow man with hawkish eyes, a voice like a blade, and a mind quick enough to cut stone.

He held Isaac's submitted problem set at arm's length, frowning.

"This is your work?" Barrow asked. It sounded more like a statement than a question.

"Yes, sir," Isaac said, sure of his work yet curious about the conversation.

"You derived Proposition III of Euclid without referring to the text," the chairman said.

"It seemed more natural that way," Isaac replied.

Barrow tilted his head. "You dislike Euclid?"

Isaac hesitated. "I... want to know why it works. Not just that it does."

Barrow did not smile, but his beard twitched and his eyes lingered.

"I shall be watching your progress."

By spring, the world shifted. Cambridge no longer

felt like a cage; it became an engine. The friction still burned, but now it drove him.

He wrote until dawn, redrawing Kepler's models with charcoal on the stone floor. He imagined bodies falling from towers, from mountaintops, from the edge of the world. He puzzled over motion—not just the act of movement, but the reason behind its changes.

"What resists change?"

"What sustains it?"

"Why does a thing keep moving when nothing touches it?"

The pieces gathered like iron filings toward an unseen magnet.

One windless night, lying beneath the crooked rafters of his garret, he watched the moon through the crack in the roof. It moved but never fell. And yet, was that not what falling was, a curve sustained forever?

He sat bolt upright, breath frozen.

"The moon falls," he whispered. "Always. But never lands."

His candle tumbled, unlit. He fumbled in the dark, heart racing, and found his notebook by touch.

The same force, he wrote, *governs apples and orbits. The law is universal. The heavens are not simply divine. They are governed by laws like everything else. And we can know how.*

Beneath that crooked beam, with ink on his fingers and wonder in his chest, Isaac Newton faced the terrifying joy of truth: the universe was not unknowable.

It was waiting to be understood.

6

—————

THE YEAR OF THE MIRROR

*W*oolsthorpe Manor, Lincolnshire—Summer 1665 to Spring 1666

The black banners went up like accusations. Cambridge closed its doors to the plague with the same quiet finality as a coffin lid. The bells of Great St. Mary's no longer rang for lectures or Matins. Instead, they tolled the names of those who would not return. Lists of the dead fluttered on chapel doors, the ink bleeding in the damp. Many professors fled. Streets emptied. The porter, who once scolded late students, now wore black cloth across his mouth and eyes like a penitent.

Isaac Newton packed a single trunk.

He did not say goodbye.

The wind struck the manor as if it had missed him.

Woolsthorpe was unchanged, yet not. The sheep still bleated across the hills. The thatched roof still creaked with every gust.

But Isaac no longer belonged here, not entirely. With the London-printed pages folded in his bag, the prisms wrapped in flannel, and the fever of mathematics in his blood, he was a stranger to the place of his boyhood.

Inside, the house was rigid with order. His mother, Hannah, kept the hearth swept and the pewter gleaming. There was no affection in the cleanliness, only control, as if she could scrub grief from the corners or polish love into existence. Isaac nodded politely in response to her inquiries and retreated upstairs.

His old room, high under the sloped eaves, smelled of lavender and moths. The leaded-glass window faced east, where the morning sun struck the frost like fire.

He unpacked as if performing a ceremony. Not clothes, but ideas: the prisms, his compass, notes written in cramped, furious script. He smoothed each page on the desk and stacked them like scripture. Then he listened — to the wind, to the clock ticking hollowly downstairs, to the space between thoughts where Cambridge's noise had once crowded out questions.

In the silence, he began.

In late summer, the grass curled dry beneath his bare feet. Bees drifted slowly between clover tufts. A cloud cast long shadows over the pasture, dulling the color of the hedgerows. Isaac leaned back against the bark of the old apple tree, sketchbook limp in his lap.

Then, an apple dropped.

Not dramatic.

Not theatrical.

Just a thump in the grass beside him.

He turned to look. Its path had not been perfectly straight. It curved, obeying something. The Earth called to it, and it had obeyed.

Not because it was light. Not because it was ripe.

Because it had to.

"What draws it?" Isaac whispered, pressing his fingers to his temple. "What calls it down?"

His pencil moved almost before the thought had fully formed.

"What if it is not the apple falling," he muttered, "but Earth pulling? What if... the Moon stays above because it is falling sideways?"

The hair on his arms lifted.

Not madness.

A pull.

Something ancient and invisible, and suddenly everywhere.

By October, rain beat hard against the window-panes. The sky wept until the soil clung to boots in heavy clumps.

Isaac transformed his room into a laboratory. He borrowed glassware from neighbors and paid a glazier to make lenses. His mother only watched him carry the pieces through the house with raised brows but said nothing. It was easier to let her think it was chemistry. It was easier not to explain.

He waited for full sunlight. On the clearest afternoon in weeks, it came — a beam of gold piercing the cloud-quiet gray.

He set the prism carefully on the sill.

Light struck.

And split.

It fractured, no, it unwound, into red, orange, yellow, green, blue, indigo, and violet across the wall like a living equation.

Isaac blinked. He moved the prism. Again, color. Again, order. Then, daringly, he introduced a second prism.

He expected chaos.

He expected noise.

Instead, white.

He gasped at his understanding. His hand knocked over the candle. Wax spilled down the table. Ink bled. He did not care. He had just seen something unknown in the world.

"Color is not distortion," he breathed. "It is... structure."

He scratched the term onto the margin of a half-used page: *spectrum.*

Something bloomed behind his ribs.

Not pride.

Not discovery.

Clarity.

And clarity would not be welcomed.

NIGHT DESCENDED EARLY in the manor, but Isaac's mind never dimmed.

He scratched circles into the wooden planks. Built tracks to roll marbles. Fashioned slings to launch small lead spheres across his chamber. A pendulum, strung from the beam, swung until its arc carved time in the air.

His mother asked once if he was well. He barely responded. Food went cold by his door.

What was friction?

What resisted motion?

What continued it?

He wrote down what he suspected:

"A body in motion remains in motion unless acted upon."

Then: "Force equals mass times acceleration."

And finally: "For every action, there is an equal and opposite reaction."

Three lines. Yet they came not with fanfare or pronouncement, but more like whispers.

As though nature herself had passed a secret, quietly and firmly, and he, at last, had listened.

March crept in cold and wet. The fields were gray, and the sheep bleated like ghosts.

A letter arrived, the seal smudged by drizzle. Barrow's handwriting slanted forward like a man in haste: "Mr. Newton, I do not doubt you have been thinking. When the world reopens, I expect you will return with no shortage of papers. But consider your audience before you make too much of your solitude."

Isaac smiled for the first time in weeks. Not because it was praise; Barrow gave little of that, but because it acknowledged what he now knew with terrible certainty: this was not idleness. This was a transformation.

"It is not solitude," he said softly to no one. "It is my laboratory." At night, he walked alone in the pasture. The stars were crisp, the wind sharp with the bite of coming frost. He held a slate and a stick of chalk, both cold in his hands. Beneath his boots, the grass crunched faintly with every step. Silence wrapped around him, save for the distant rustle of trees and the occasional hoot of an owl.

Above, the Moon drifted across the sky in her slow, measured arc, always returning to him as if she, too, pondered the same questions. It always came back to her. Not just light and beauty, but motion. Why did she not fall? Why did she not fly away?

He turned the slate in his hand, chalk tapping rhythmically against its surface. He worked the numbers again: gravitational pull, centripetal force, orbital velocity. Ratios and relationships danced through his mind. The same force that pulled the apple down, could it reach so far? Could it pull the Moon?

Each calculation brought him closer. Each refinement tightened the invisible string that bound sky to earth. What if this force had no end? What if the apple and the Moon were tied by the same unseen law?

He paused and looked up, breath fogging in the chill air. The Moon hung serene, indifferent to his speculation. And yet, she moved with purpose, always within reach, always on time. Not chaos, but order.

A deep thrill stirred in his chest, more than curiosity now. It was recognition, a whisper on the edge of certainty. Nature was not random; it was written in a language he was beginning to understand.

He scribbled again on the slate. A number adjusted. A radius refined. Each time, the math drew closer. Each time, the thread between apple and Moon pulled tighter. The arc of the apple became the curve of the cosmos. This attraction was not just a force; it was the quiet hand shaping the universe.

He walked on, alone beneath the stars, but no longer in the dark.

"They are the same," he whispered, breath shallow, the words barely stirring the air. "The same rule."

Awe rose in his throat like a tide, expansive, luminous, and terrible. His mind raced to keep pace with the implications, but part of him had already crossed a threshold. The veil was lifting. The universe was not a scattered collection of curiosities and coincidences. It was not chaos and miracle. It was unity. Cohesion. Precision.

And something else stirred inside him now, just behind the awe. Dread.

If this was true, if the force that tugged the apple to the earth also held the Moon in her arc, turned the tides, and pulled the stars in their sweeping courses, then the world was no longer an infinite mystery. It was not separate things behaving by chance.

It was one thing. One machine. One rhythm. One law. And it had waited, silent and invisible, for centuries to be noticed.

He stopped walking. The pasture stretched out before him in silvered darkness. Above, the stars wheeled slowly along ancient paths. All of it, each flicker, each motion, part of the same vast engine, ticking with perfect indifference.

For the first time, he felt the full weight of what it meant to understand. Not just to guess or glimpse, but to truly know.

To see the world laid bare, no longer enchanted, but governed.

And yet, in that starkness, there was also beauty— a kind of sacred order. Not less miraculous, but more so.

He stood motionless for a long time, slate forgotten at his side, eyes fixed on the sky.

The universe was speaking.

And at last, someone was listening.

By spring, lambs cried in the far fields, and Isaac's notebooks bulged like lungs filling with breath.

He had one on optics. Another on motion. And a third, hidden beneath a floorboard, on attraction.

"The force of attraction diminishes with the square of distance," he wrote. "The inverse square law."

He sketched a cannonball on his slate—simple, solid, a sphere of iron and force. Then he slowly drew the Earth beneath it. He imagined the ball fired from a mountaintop, faster and faster, until it fell so far and so fast that it never touched the ground, its fall bending with the curvature of the world. Falling forever. An orbit.

The idea struck him like lightning—not loud or violent, but total, seizing his entire mind in a quiet, burning clarity. He stared at the drawing, not for what it was, but for what it meant. The cannonball was no longer just a thought experiment. It was the Moon. It was every planet. It was everything that moved in the heavens.

And once the image took root, it would not leave. It clung behind his eyes, imprinted like the afterimage of the sun. Even when he slept, it hovered just out of reach, its logic whispering through his dreams.

Later, he would call this time his *Annus Mirabilis*, his Year of Wonders—a year in which the universe unfolded beneath his fingertips. Gravitation. Motion. Optics. Calculus. As if the laws had always been written, and now, at last, the ink was drying where he had traced their form.

But at the moment, there were no choirs. No accolades. No ovations or crowded halls. Genius, it turned out, did not arrive with trumpets. Only the soft flutter of parchment catching the draft from the shuttered window. Only the hiss of candlelight burning down to the wick in the silence of midnight. Only ink-stained hands trembling, not from cold, but from the unbearable clarity of what he now saw.

The universe was not distant. It was not unknowable. It could be written, measured, predicted. It could be held. And it had waited centuries for someone not to praise it, but to see it.

He exhaled, the faintest smile tugging at his lips, though tears stung the corners of his eyes. Not from sorrow, and not entirely from joy, but from something deeper—reverence.

He was alone, yet never again in the dark.

The universe was not unknowable.

It had always been speaking.

He had finally learned to listen.

7

THE RELUCTANT SUN

ambridge University, Trinity College — 1667
The air in Cambridge smelled of ink and tobacco, of damp stone darkened by centuries of drizzle and footsteps, and of something older still—resentment, perhaps, or tradition dressed in its ceremonial robes. It was the kind of smell that clings to long corridors and older minds, heavy with expectation and heavier still with memory.

Isaac returned in the autumn. Not with fanfare or titles, but with crates and boxes—stacked, weathered, filled with the silent weight of notebooks. Pages upon pages of diagrams, equations, theorems, and corrections, scratched out and rewritten with obsessive care. He brought no entourage, only the ink on his sleeves and the calluses on his fingers.

His hands were stained with the colors of light, quite literally, residue from his work with prisms and lenses. His eyes were ringed with the deep shadows of sleepless nights, the kind born not from worry but from thought—dense, relentless thought. He walked the old paths of Trinity like a man returning from a long voyage, not just in distance but in understanding.

There was something otherworldly in his posture now, a quiet tension in the way he carried himself, as if still half-living in another realm—a realm where truth reigned, not rank; where equations spoke more clearly than titles; where ideas were not inherited but earned.

He wore his old academic robe. It was patched, faded at the cuffs, and frayed at the hem. But he wore it not from humility, nor from nostalgia, but because he did not care about refinement. What he had touched, what he knew, did not need the approval of gowns or dinners or societies.

He passed through the gate of Trinity College with the quiet precision of someone aware of everything— the creak of the hinges, the worn path beneath his feet, the echo of his own steps. He measured them all without meaning to. Habit, or maybe reverence.

He was twenty-four, and he had already learned to mistrust applause. It came too easily to those who had solved too little.

It was in the chapel cloister that Professor Isaac Barrow found him. The cloister was cold, light filtering through leaded glass in quiet ribbons. Barrow's beard had grown whiter since Isaac had last seen him, but his presence had not diminished. He still moved with the lean precision of a man used to cutting through fog, intellectual or otherwise.

His eyes, though, were the same—sharp, patient. Not welcoming, but weighing. Like a sword testing whether the sheath still fit. He said nothing for a long moment, simply studying the young man before him. The silence stretched, respectful and unhurried.

"You look," Barrow said at last, his voice low and amused, "as though you've been listening to the stars."

Isaac's gaze did not waver. "I have," he said softly.

Barrow's brow lifted, only slightly. "And what have they said?"

Isaac looked past him then, to the window and the pale daylight beyond.

"That they obey," he whispered, "the same laws as apples."

For a heartbeat, nothing moved. Even the air seemed to still. Barrow blinked once, then smiled— not out of politeness, but from a place deeper, older. A rare, quiet smile.

He did not ask for proof. He did not doubt.

He knew the boy had not returned the same.

The lecture hall was a place of firewood and formality. Rows of students sat in their black gowns, arms folded. The air smelled of stale bread, ink, and damp wool. A young Newton stood before them with his hand on a single object: a glass prism, catching the slanting light of the window.

He waited until the murmurs faded.

"I shall show you," he said, "that white light is not singular, but composed of many colors, each refracted at its own degree."

They scoffed, especially Edward Lucas, a senior scholar with the voice of a preacher and the pride of a noble.

"Are we to replace the firm light of Heaven," Lucas asked, "with rainbows and witchcraft?"

Isaac only turned the prism slowly.

The beam struck.

The wall bloomed into violet, indigo, blue, green, yellow, orange, red.

The hall fell into stunned silence.

Then a cough.

Then a ripple of unease.

Not because they doubted it.

But because it changed everything.

Barrow arranged for Isaac to present his findings to

the senior fellows. They came in small groups, men with Latin tongues and long memories. Isaac showed them his experiments—his optics, his calculations of motion and force. Always with care. Always reluctant.

He preferred speaking with chalk on a blackboard rather than meeting their eyes. When he spoke of a universal attractive force, one professor shook his head.

"You speak of a force acting through a vacuum? An invisible hand that stretches across space and touches the Moon?"

"I speak of what the numbers reveal," Isaac answered.

"But what causes this force?"

"I do not presume to say."

That, more than anything, unsettled them. He was not trying to please. He was trying to know.

By candlelight, he wrote in tight, furious lines—diagrams of orbits, ellipses, triangles with Greek letters and measurements. He muttered as he worked.

"If the sun ceased to shine... would the Earth fly straight?... No. It would keep curving. It would follow its last command."

He stared at the flame.

The world, he believed, was not held up by angels.

It moved because motion demanded it.

It curved because space allowed it.

It obeyed not men, not kings, not bishops, but law. And that law was written in the language of mathematics.

Word began to spread—not just through Cambridge, but to London, to the Royal Society, to Hooke, who had once drawn spirals of planetary motion.

"Newton?" Hooke wrote. "A promising man. But he builds on my ideas."

Isaac's hands trembled when he read that. Not because he feared Hooke, but because he knew how easily truth could be claimed by others, bent by ego, twisted by power.

He did not want fame.

He wanted the freedom to think.

But now he could feel the tide of attention turning toward him.

In 1667, Isaac was elected a Fellow. A narrow bed and a key to a room with frost-bitten panes and a fire that never stayed lit. He had the freedom to think, to write, to teach.

In 1669, Barrow did something remarkable.

He resigned his position as Lucasian Professor of Mathematics.

And named Isaac Newton his successor.

At twenty-six, Isaac stood before the Board of Electors, his notebook trembling in his coat pocket.

"Do you accept the appointment?" one asked.

Isaac nodded.

"But I will not publish," he said.

The man laughed. "We'll see."

That night, back in his room, Isaac sat by the dying coals. The walls were stone, but they seemed to breathe with heat and age. He stared into the fire.

He had not asked for recognition.

But now he had authority.

He whispered his laws aloud, first slowly, then with confidence. Each one was measured not just in force and mass, but in clarity.

A body remains at rest...

Force equals change in motion...

Every action...

Each word steadied him. Each phrase drove away the ghosts of isolation and doubt.

He was no longer the boy building clocks from scraps.

He was the man defining motion itself.

And yet, part of him still longed for Woolsthorpe, for the orchard, for the quiet. The world of men, he knew, would never be as orderly as the arc of a falling apple.

Isaac took his findings to the Royal Society, seeking the attention they required.

The hallway was narrow and dim, lined with portraits of dead men whose names carried weight in the Society, their painted eyes seeming to watch every disagreement unfold beneath them.

Isaac Newton's footsteps echoed quietly as he turned the corner, a stack of papers in his arms containing his latest treatise on the nature of light. He had barely crossed into the corridor when he stopped short.

Robert Hooke was there, leaning against the wall beneath a sconce, his arms crossed. His sharp, weathered face twisted into something like a smirk.

"Newton," he sneered. "I see you've brought more papers to dazzle the Society."

Isaac stiffened. "I've submitted a letter about my experiments with prisms. The evidence is clear."

Hooke pushed off the wall and stepped closer. "Clear to you, perhaps. But I've done work on light myself, long before your Cambridge optics. You're not the first man to claim an understanding of its nature."

"I've never claimed to be," Newton said coldly. "But if my findings contradict yours, perhaps it is the data that deserves judgment, not the ego."

Hooke's eyes narrowed. "Your data bends light into

neat little rainbows and calls it truth. But light is a wave, not particles skipping through the air like stones. And no amount of mirrors or prisms will make it otherwise."

Newton's grip on his papers tightened. His heart beat hard in his chest. He hated this—the heat of confrontation—but something inside him would not let him retreat.

"I've measured the angles precisely," he said, forcing calm. "The colors separate not because of the glass itself, but because white light is composed of all colors. That is not theory; it is demonstration."

"And yet," Hooke said, stepping closer, "you fail to acknowledge the foundation others laid—my *Micrographia*, for example. You act as if the world began with your vision."

"I act as if truth matters more than pride," Newton snapped, louder than he intended.

The corridor grew quiet. Footsteps paused in the adjoining room. Hooke's jaw clenched, but he only gave a tight, brittle smile.

"Be careful, Newton," he said. "Brilliance is no shield against the politics of this place. The Royal Society is not your laboratory to command."

"And it is not your stage to dominate," Newton shot back.

For a long moment, neither man moved. The silence between them was thick, less a pause than a drawing of battle lines.

Then Hooke turned and walked away, his footsteps clipped and sharp.

Newton remained alone beneath the painted eyes of old philosophers. He exhaled slowly, his shoulders tense. He hated arguments. But worse, he hated silence in the face of error.

He turned, straightened his papers, and walked toward the meeting room, his jaw set, the bitterness still clinging to him like dust.

Neither man had won. But they had each made it clear: they would never stand on common ground.

8

THE WEIGHT OF THE WORLD

ambridge, 1684

Rain tapped steadily against the tall, leaded windowpanes of Newton's rooms at Trinity College, painting the glass with drifting rivulets that blurred the already gray world outside. The air inside carried the mingled scents of tallow, old parchment, and a faint trace of sulfur from long-forgotten experiments. Beneath his bare feet, the wooden floor was cold enough to sting.

Isaac Newton stood at the window, shoulders stiff, jaw set, eyes unfocused on the college courtyard below.

In his hand, he held a letter, creased, smudged, and reread so many times it had grown soft as cloth along the edges. His thumb moved over the lines again, almost without thought.

"Dear Sir, I beg of you, what curve would a planet describe if it were drawn by a force inversely proportional to the square of its distance?"

Newton's lips barely moved, yet the words were etched inside him now. Edmond Halley's question was not new to him. He had known the answer for years, perhaps since the lonely plague years in Woolsthorpe when time itself had seemed to slow to a crawl and the universe whispered its secrets to anyone patient enough to listen.

But knowing something and speaking it aloud for others to hear were not the same.

With a slow breath, he folded the letter and placed it among a scatter of yellowed notes, half-finished diagrams, and the shattered stub of a graphite stylus. Outside, the cloister bell tolled, distant and hollow.

He had always known this moment would come.

Halley arrived with the rain, his presence as brisk and kinetic as a summer gust blown in from London. His boots clattered across the stone steps, his cloak dripping rivulets onto the floor as the porter hesitated before letting him through. Halley was all movement, all conversation, his reputation as a wit and adventurer preceding him. He had charted southern stars, predicted comets, argued politics with courtiers and sailors alike. Where Newton preferred to stay in the shadows, Halley enjoyed the fire of debate.

Newton opened the door before the knock landed.

"Isaac," Halley said, breathless, his eyes alight. "I've come for the orbit."

Newton stepped aside without a word. The chamber was dim, lit only by a smoking oil lamp and a thin sliver of afternoon light. Scrolls and folios were stacked haphazardly, spilling into corners and climbing across shelves. There was no fire. No food. The room was as severe as its master.

"You have it, don't you?" Halley asked, shaking water from his cloak. "You've solved the inverse-square law?"

"I worked it out once," Newton replied, his voice low, guarded. "During the plague years. But the paper is misplaced."

"Misplaced?" Halley's voice rose, then steadied. He studied Newton's face, the way his eyes darted away from contact. "But you remember it."

Newton crossed to the desk, sorting through a heap of papers until his fingers found a worn folio bound with a faded red cord. He opened it carefully, revealing a scattering of geometrical sketches, annotations in Latin, and the clean arcs of planetary ellipses.

Halley exhaled sharply, reverently. "By God. You did."

Newton's expression did not change. "It's not for public debate."

Halley's hands closed around the parchment like a man handling relics. He had braved seas and tempests, yet here was a discovery that shook him more than any storm. "But you must write it. Complete it. This is the key. The key to the heavens."

Newton's gaze shifted to the darkened window. Outside, a gust of wind rattled the panes. "They won't understand. Or worse, they'll pretend they already did."

Halley studied him for a long moment. He saw what few men ever did — Newton's brilliance, yes, but also his suspicion, his loneliness, his gnawing fear of ridicule. The world had mocked him once, and he had withdrawn like a wounded animal. Now Halley knew he must coax him back out, not with flattery, but with insistence.

"This is bigger than they are," Halley said quietly. "Bigger than us both. You cannot let it rot in these chambers."

For days after Halley left, Newton did not sleep. Not truly. He drifted in and out of reverie, waking at odd hours with his mind brimming with calculations.

The universe had become a fever in him again, burning just behind the eyes.

In the silence of the college, broken only by the strike of the chapel bell or the rustle of students in the halls, he began to write.

By candlelight, he scratched lines across parchment until his wrist ached. Diagrams unfurled like living things: ellipses, parabolas, triangles nested within spheres. He muttered aloud as he worked.

"Every body continues in its state of rest, or uniform motion in a straight line..."

Words and numbers wove together like scripture.

He scarcely noticed the cold. He scarcely noticed the ache in his stomach or the numbness in his toes. Time no longer moved forward; it circled around him in arcs, governed by laws he was only now beginning to understand.

The stars did not wander aimlessly, he realized. They obeyed. And if they obeyed, they could be known.

Halley returned in November, his face red from wind and news.

"Hooke has heard whispers," he said without greeting. "He is claiming credit."

Newton turned from the blackboard, chalk still in hand. "Then let him publish his proof."

Halley laughed without humor. "He has no proof. Only pride."

"Then I will give them proof," Newton said softly. "Not to disprove Hooke, but to set the record straight."

He opened a cabinet and drew out the stack of completed folios. Three volumes now, bound with string, ink still drying in places. It was not a book yet, but it was close.

Halley's eyes shone with something like triumph. He understood in that instant that his role was not merely that of a messenger, but of midwife to a work that would change how mankind saw the universe. Newton would not have given it freely. Halley had pried it out of him with persistence, with faith, with the conviction that truth deserved daylight.

As winter deepened, the manuscript grew heavy with attraction and motion and unyielding logic. Each law emerged like a chisel mark across stone, shaping the rough matter of thought into something precise and enduring.

Newton whispered as he wrote.

"To every action, an equal and opposite reaction..."

He imagined forces stretching invisibly between stars, binding them to one another. The same force that pulled an apple to the ground held the planets to the sun. The same rules everywhere.

The symmetry struck him with almost perfect clarity.

In the spring of 1687, the *Principia* was completed.

Halley, ever the faithful emissary, arranged the printing himself. When the Royal Society pled poverty, he offered his own purse. Newton refused dedications; he would not flatter kings or cardinals.

"This is not a work of homage," he said. "It is a work of truth."

Word spread quickly, carried by whispers and sharp-edged letters. Some read it with wonder. Others scoffed. Robert Hooke fumed with accusations.

"He stole my ideas," Hooke claimed.

Newton remained silent. He had expected the noise, but the work was now beyond reach.

Let the world argue.

He had said what needed saying.

On a clear night, not long after the first copies were bound, Newton walked alone through the college grounds. Frost shimmered silver across the grass under the moonlight.

He paused beneath the chapel arch, looked upward, and breathed.

The stars above did not twinkle. Not to him. They burned steadily, constantly, patient.

He closed his eyes.

He thought of Woolsthorpe, of the orchard and the windmill, of long hours watching shadows cross walls and measuring water drips with a child's precision. He had once been a boy chasing silence. Now silence followed him.

He whispered to the sky, his voice low and steady.

"Every body continues in its state…"

"Force equals the change in motion…"

"To every action…"

Each phrase anchored him. He was no longer the boy beneath the apple tree. He was the man who had given names to the motions of the heavens. And he had done it not for glory, but because the universe had asked a question. And someone had to answer.

9

SHADOWS OF LIGHT

ambridge, 1688

The fire snapped in protest as Newton prodded it with an iron poker. Sparks leapt upward, disappearing into the soot-darkened chimney. He sought neither warmth nor the comfort of light against winter's deep grip. What he sought was motion. A resistance to stillness. Something that kept his body from collapsing into dust, like the pages scattered around him.

His chambers were crowded now, overrun with glass prisms, hand-ground lenses, and sealed flasks. Shadows stretched and recoiled across the walls in the flickering firelight. The *Principia* had gone out to the world, and to his astonishment, the world had come back to him. Letters. Praise. Dissent.

More than he cared to answer.

He turned instead to optics. The prism called him back. Morning light streamed through the tall windows and split cleanly through the glass prism, which hung from a string like a crystal pendulum. Colors spilled across the table, a vibrant spectrum that wavered and shimmered with the movement of the air.

He adjusted the angle. Again. Measured the spread with calipers. Again.

"Not a corruption of light," he whispered. "But a composition."

He reached for his notebook; the leather cracked and worn from years of use. He sketched what he saw, then filled the margins in his crabbed, slanted hand: *The colored light is not altered by the glass but separated. Each hue has a distinct angle of refraction.*

The prism revealed what the eye could not.

A knock interrupted him. Not the timid rap of a student, but firm and assured.

He opened the door to find John Locke.

"You look like a man haunted," Locke said, stepping in without waiting.

Newton closed the door behind him, more startled than annoyed. "I am haunted. But not by spirits."

They sat over bread and clotted cream, the remains of an untouched breakfast. Newton pushed a cup of water toward Locke but did not pour for himself.

Locke, keen-eyed and deliberate in his movements, studied him. "Your *Principia* has stirred minds in Oxford and London," he said. "But it has also unsettled them."

"I did not write to comfort."

"No," Locke allowed, "but comfort is the ground most men wish to stand upon. You pull it away. You make the world mechanical. Predictable. Stripped of mystery."

Newton glanced at the prism, its colors fading as the sun shifted.

"Then they should look closer," he said. "There is beauty in the design. The elegance of it."

Locke leaned forward. "But beauty does not console the common man. Nor the magistrate, nor the clergyman. They ask, where is God in your laws? If nature obeys your equations, is the Almighty reduced to a distant watchmaker?"

Newton's gaze sharpened. "God is the architect. Not absent. Not idle. The laws are His handiwork. He upholds them moment by moment."

Locke considered him, lips pressed thin. "And yet if all is law, where is liberty? Where is the freedom of the human soul? I spend my days defending the rights of men, and you would fold us into the same equations that govern falling stones."

Newton's jaw tightened. "Stones do not reason. Men do. Reason itself is proof of design."

"Design, yes," Locke said, "but not dominion. God gave us faculties to use, not merely to calculate."

Their words hung heavy between them. They were contemporaries, two men of the same century, breathing the same air, yet orbiting different stars. Locke, a philosopher of men and governments, sought a middle ground between faith and freedom. Newton, a philosopher of nature, demanded order, precision, certainty.

The prism caught a shaft of light and scattered it across the wall. Locke turned toward it.

"And this?" he asked. "You say light itself is divisible, a composite of colors. But I ask, is the eye not deceived? Does perception itself not make truth slippery?"

Newton answered without hesitation. "The prism proves it. White is not pure but mixed. Red bends least. Violet most. Sight is not deception, but revelation, if one looks with care."

Locke's brow furrowed. "Yet if reality is filtered through the mind, how can we claim certainty? All knowledge begins in experience, in the senses. And senses can falter."

Newton's voice grew sharp. "Then experiment again. Correct the error. Truth is not lost because men are careless in looking."

Locke allowed himself a small smile. "Ever the absolutist. I say truth must be held lightly, for it comes to us through fallible vessels. You say truth is a fortress."

"It is," Newton said flatly. "And I have built its walls in ink and proof."

That night, after Locke departed, Newton returned to his telescope. The air was bitter, frost edging the stone sill. His breath plumed in silver clouds, but the stars above were clear. Distant. Constant.

He adjusted the focus, turned the brass dial, and brought the moon into crisp relief. Craters, ridges, shadows. Not smooth. Not perfect. Like man. Like himself.

In the quiet, he remembered Woolsthorpe, the attic, the grinding of lenses in secret, the thrill of a star slipping into view. He had always wanted to see farther.

In February, a letter arrived from the Royal Society. Sir Robert Hooke had died. Newton held the paper in his hand for a long while. No smile. No triumph. Only a slow breath.

Hooke had been more than a rival. He had been a thorn, a voice forever questioning, accusing, demanding credit. For years, Newton had felt his shadow pressing against every word he wrote. Now the shadow was gone.

The tension in his shoulders eased. A door, once barred, now stood open. He would be offered the presidency. He did not yet know whether he would accept. But he did know this: Hooke's absence felt less like victory, and more like the sudden quiet that follows thunder. For the first time, the past seemed still.

The air softened. Trees in the courtyard bloomed pale green. Students lounged on the grass in scattered circles, laughing and tossing small stones in idle competition.

Newton passed them unnoticed, a shadow in a dark coat. He made his way to the chapel. Not to pray. To sit.

The stained glass cast fractured light across the stone floor, tiny spectrums shifting with each passing cloud.

He closed his eyes. In the dark behind his eyelids, he imagined the colors combining pure white. Into unity. He saw, at last, not chaos. But design.

10

SHADOWS AND SPECTRA

ondon, 1691

The candle sputtered on the edge of extinguishing, its wax pooling into a warped lake across the desk. Newton sat hunched in the back room of his Leicester Fields residence, right hand streaked with silver nitrate, left gripping a quill. The house was silent but for the faint creak of beams above and the scurry of mice in the walls. Outside, frost spread across the panes like veins of cold light.

He had not slept in two days. His hair, once tied with care, now fell loose and wild over his shoulders. His eyes, hollowed from fatigue, flicked between pages of notes and the prisms scattered before him. Light bent, split, reflected. It danced across the walls in fleeting arcs of color as he tilted a single pane of glass.

He was no longer merely a mathematician or astronomer. He hunted the very composition of light itself.

A knock startled him.

Not for its volume; it was soft, almost polite, but because it came without warning.

Newton trained himself to expect patterns: footsteps in the stairwell, the hush of cloth against stone, the groan of a floorboard. This broke the stillness like stone striking water.

He stood abruptly, stool scraping against the floor. The sudden motion unbalanced him; his knee struck the desk. The quill slipped from his fingers, falling with a delicate scratch across the grain of oak.

"Who is it?" he called, sharp with irritation to mask surprise.

A pause. Then a voice, familiar, warm, muffled by the oak: "It's me. Fatio."

Newton let out a breath through his nose, more pressure than sound. He steadied himself against the desk, then moved to the door with deliberate slowness. The latch clicked cold under his hand.

When the door opened, lamplight spilled in, catching chalk dust suspended in the air. Snowflakes melted on Nicolas Fatio de Duillier's shoulders, glittering like salt before vanishing. His cheeks were flushed from the cold, his lips parting as he adjusted to the warmth.

"You look worse than last time," Fatio said, a smirk curling his wind-bitten mouth.

Newton offered no smile. He turned back to his desk, robe swaying behind him like a curtain pulled in haste.

"That's the price of insight," he murmured.

Fatio stepped inside, brushing off his sleeves. "Or obsession," he said, dropping his satchel with a thump. The scent of winter clung to him: cold air, faint smoke, damp wool.

They spoke late into the night. Candles guttered low, casting long shadows across shelves crowded with instruments and books. Ink glistened in half-dried pools on the desk. A kettle, long forgotten, cooled on the hearth.

Fatio leaned over Newton's diagrams, curls falling like shadows across the parchment. His finger traced the dense Latin notes and angles too precise for common eyes.

"YOU STILL HOLD that light is corpuscular?" he asked, voice curious more than confrontational.

Newton nodded, sipping tea gone bitter.

"I see no reason to doubt it. Waves do not travel in straight lines. These shadows, sharp, clean, bear no trace of undulation."

Fatio tilted his head. "Yet waves cannot be ruled out. Dispersion, interference... they whisper of something softer, something fluid."

"Waves cannot be weighed," Newton said flatly. "I'll believe in ether when I can measure it."

Fatio's mouth twitched. "You measure everything. Even people."

The words hung in the air like a struck tuning fork. Newton said nothing. He looked at his notes, then away. He would not argue that. Not tonight.

There was something in Fatio Newton trusted. More than trust, he enjoyed him, in the rare, cautious way Newton allowed himself to enjoy anyone. Fatio's mind was agile, unburdened by the need to impress. He did not flinch when challenged, nor flatter where flattery might rot the conversation. His admiration was genuine, but never servile.

Newton, who had bricked himself into solitude stone by stone, found this young Swiss mathematician slipping through the cracks like light itself. Closer than anyone since his boyhood in Grantham.

Fatio carried no envy, and Newton, in these dim-lit

hours, wore no mask. For once, the great mind of England, so often whispered of with reverence or suspicion, allowed himself simply to be.

A man in a room with another who understood. Later, as the fire sank low, Newton stared into the coals.

"I have been offered the Wardenship of the Mint," he said.

Fatio looked up sharply. "You? A government post?"

"I'd take it. My work at Cambridge is done. In London, I could control more."

"Control what?"

Newton's voice dropped. "Truth. Justice. Fraud. The alchemist's poison knowledge, the counterfeiter's poison coin. It is all corruption, all falsity, all decay."

Fatio studied him. "You would make a dreadful politician."

"I have no interest in politics," Newton said, rising to snuff the candle. "Only purification."

The Royal Mint, Tower of London, 1696

The clang of hammer against die was ceaseless. The air was thick with sweat, metal filings, and coal soot. Newton stood in the coining room, sleeves rolled, boots damp with blackened water. Here, beneath fortress walls older than memory, he confronted another problem.

Counterfeiters.

Men who shaved silver, clipped coins, debased crowns. They undermined the nation's currency and, to Newton, the very fabric of empirical order.

He tracked them methodically, sending spies into taverns, hiring agents, studying dies and signatures with the same meticulous eye he turned on optics.

At trial, his tone was clinical.

"They forged the inscription. The pressure marks on the rim show filing. This man is guilty."

One by one, they were convicted.

Some hanged. Newton did not flinch.

Fatio visited less. Each was consumed with work, and Newton noticed the distance, though he said nothing. He filled the silence with drafts on color, letters to philosophers abroad, notes on the elusive "philosopher's mercury" he still believed might transmute base metals.

He no longer spoke of alchemy openly, too many eyes, but he still believed in it. Not for gold. For purity. For divine order.

One winter morning, he returned home to a letter from Fatio. Apologetic. He had been offered a commission abroad. He would go. He hoped Newton would understand.

Newton sat by the window, the letter trembling in his fingers. He did not reply. That night, he added a line to his notebook: *Even light, once broken, cannot be made whole again.*

11

THE DREAM OF UNITY

ondon, 1697

L   The clatter of hooves in the courtyard rose like a mechanical heartbeat. Rain spattered against the windows of Newton's study in Tower Green, blurring the view of the Thames into shifting gray ribbons. Inside, coal smoke and candle wax hung in the air, softening the outlines of books, brass instruments, and teetering stacks of parchment.

Newton stood at the far window, his narrow figure a silhouette against the dim afternoon light. He watched the raindrops trace crooked lines down the glass. Even chaos followed law, he thought. Surely even rain must obey its hidden rules.

Behind him, the fire cracked. A voice broke the silence, clear but quiet.

"You should eat."

Newton turned, blinking as though waking. His clerk Humphrey stood in the doorway, pale and stiff, a boy who already looked worn by ink and duty.

"I am not hungry," Newton murmured.

"You haven't eaten since yesterday."

Newton waved him off, moving toward the desk piled with diagrams, ellipses, parabolas, curves of stars and comets, each a step toward binding the heavens to the earth. Humphrey retreated, leaving him to the night and his endless proofs.

THE NEXT MORNING brought a disturbance Newton did not expect. A woman waited in the drawing room.

He entered cautiously, boots silent on the floorboards. There she was: tall, cloaked, auburn curls streaked with silver, eyes bright with purpose.

"Catherine Barton," he said. His voice almost cracked.

His niece rose. "Uncle Isaac."

It had been years. She had shed the awe of childhood and carried herself with confidence now. Her smile carried both fondness and appraisal, as though she were measuring the man as carefully as his equations.

"You live like a ghost," she said, brushing soot from her glove.

"I live efficiently." He feebly explained.

"You're forty-five." She countered.

"Forty-four," he corrected.

Catherine smirked. "Then still young enough to learn how to dine with humans."

That afternoon they walked the damp paths of Tower Green, gulls wheeling like restless scribbles against the sky. Newton carried a folded umbrella, though he hardly noticed the drizzle as he lectured.

"Comets are not wanderers," he said. "Their paths are precise, governed. Elliptical, parabolic. If they obey gravity, then they are not portents of doom but proof of order."

Catherine listened, then stopped him with a simple question. "And if they are both? Order, yes, but also omen? The people who look up don't measure them with compasses. They measure them in fear, in wonder. Doesn't that matter too?"

Newton frowned. "Science is not obliged to soothe superstition."

"No. But men are. And you are a man, Uncle, not a theorem."

He looked at her, startled by her insistence. Few

dared press him like this. "It is lonely work," he admitted softly.

"Then why do it alone?" she asked.

"Because I cannot trust..." He faltered.

"Fatio... others. Disappointment is a force of its own."

"Then let me be disappointed for you," Catherine said, with a gentle firmness. "And still stay."

True to her word, she stayed.

Catherine became his quiet steward, organizing papers before they toppled into chaos, reminding him to eat, coaxing him into conversation when he retreated too far into numbers. But more than that, she became his mirror, reflecting his ideas in words plain enough to test their strength.

At night, when Newton read aloud his laws — motion, force, reaction — she interrupted.

"So if I lean on this table, it leans back on me with equal force?"

"Yes."

"Then why does it not feel like a battle? Why am I not exhausted by its resistance?"

"Because the forces balance. The world persists in equilibrium."

"Then your laws are not only about struggle. They are about balance."

Newton considered this. He rarely thought of them in such human terms, but her framing settled into him like a seed.

IN THE WEEKS THAT FOLLOWED, he worked with a new rhythm. Corresponding with Halley, Flamsteed. Testing pendulums, charting Jupiter's moons. Catherine often stood by, challenging his abstractions.

"If the same force pulls the moon and an apple, then you're saying the heavens are no different from my kitchen garden."

"Yes."

"Then your discovery is not only great, it is dangerous. You're pulling God down from the sky, putting Him into cabbages."

Newton's lips tightened. "I am showing the laws He set in motion. That honors Him."

"It may. Or it may frighten those who need the sky to stay mysterious."

Her words grounded him, even as they unsettled. They reminded him of the world beyond proofs, the people who must one day live with them.

.   .   .

ONE SLEEPLESS NIGHT, Newton paced the Tower walls. The stars broke through the drifting clouds, cold fires in an endless dark.

He whispered into the wind: "The laws explain the how, never the why."

Behind him, Catherine's voice: "Perhaps the why isn't yours to solve. Perhaps yours is only to give the world its language, so others may seek their own answers."

He turned, surprised to see her there, wrapped in her cloak against the chill. She touched his arm, steadying him.

"History won't only remember your equations," she said. "It will remember the shape they gave to life. So shape it well."

IN THE SPRING OF 1697, Newton presented his final papers to the Royal Society. The reception was divided — praise, scorn, accusation. He bore it silently. Later, in private, he told Catherine: "Noise fades. Shape remains."

She smiled. "Then let's make sure you live long enough to enjoy the quiet."

That evening, Newton placed *Philosophiæ Naturalis*

Principia Mathematica on the shelf above his desk. Three laws. One force. A universe revealed.

He sat in the silence that followed, listening, not to applause, but to the steady rhythm of life. The crackle of fire, the scrape of Catherine turning pages nearby, the faint tick of the world itself, at last made audible.

12

THE MEASURE OF A MAN

ondon, 1727

The morning fog clung to the Thames like a shawl, curling through alleys and drifting across the river's surface with the slow certainty of time. London stirred beneath it: carts creaked over cobblestones, chimneys exhaled into the gray sky, and the bells of St. Martin's tolled the hour.

Inside a tall stone house near Leicester Fields, Isaac Newton sat quietly by the hearth. The logs had burned low, casting a soft orange glow across the paneled walls and the silver hair that framed his gaunt face. His rooms were no longer cluttered with papers and diagrams. The experiments had ceased years ago, but silence remained, silence thick enough to hear his own thoughts shifting like old dust: unsettled, yet familiar.

In his lap lay a letter. Not from a king, nor Parliament, nor the Royal Society. It was from a boy in Lincolnshire.

Sir Isaac, my name is George, and I live near Woolsthorpe. My schoolmaster says you made clocks and sundials when you were my age. Is it true? I want to be a philosopher too. Please tell me how you started.

Newton's lips curled faintly. He seldom answered such letters, but today he lifted his pen.

Dear George, he wrote, his fingers trembling only slightly. *I began with questions, not answers. The sky, the wind, the shape of shadows. They are good teachers if you are patient.*

When he set the letter aside, he lingered over the boy's name. George. A mind not yet bound by doctrine or rivalry. Perhaps one day the lad would read his words and see not just mathematics, but the living pulse of inquiry.

Later that afternoon, Newton wandered through his house alone. Servants moved softly in distant rooms, but none disturbed him. He paused at a window overlooking the garden. The yews and elms there reminded him little of Woolsthorpe's orchard, yet the pull of memory was strong.

He had returned there only once, in middle age, walking the grounds of his boyhood with deliberate steps. He stood beneath the famous apple tree, though whether it was truly the same tree he could not be sure, and felt a quiet tremor of gratitude. Gratitude for solitude, for shadow, for the long silent years that had given his mind room to roam.

As evening fell, a visitor arrived. A man in his thirties with dark hair, eyes quick as mercury, and a restless energy. John Conduitt, his assistant, his chronicler, and kin through marriage.

"You've had another letter," John said, setting down a packet. "A student at Cambridge. Claims your *Principia* changed his life. He asks what you think of Descartes."

"I think," Newton murmured dryly, "that Descartes thought too much of himself."

John laughed.

The sound stirred something unexpected in Newton, not annoyance, not melancholy. Affection, perhaps. It had taken him most of his life to understand he was loved not for his discoveries, but despite them.

That night, Newton dreamed of falling.

He was once more in the orchard. The apple tree rose before him like a cathedral, its branches heavy with memory. Above it, the sky opened wide and endless. He looked up, and instead of the apple dropping, it was he who drifted upward, drawn by the heavens rather than held by gravity.

He passed the clouds, the moon, the planets, each moving in quiet obedience to the same law. And in his dream, he wept—not from fear, but from awe.

When he woke, there were tears on his cheek.

His final days unfolded in quiet rhythms. Meals. Walks through the garden. Brief readings by candlelight. He no longer filled margins with notes or scribbled theories on scraps of paper. He was no longer at war with Hooke, or his own pride. Those battles had dissolved into dust and legacy.

Sometimes he spoke aloud, testing the familiar words, as if to reassure himself they still belonged to him: "Every body continues in its state of rest..."

He still believed it. Perhaps now more than ever.

On the evening of March 19, the pain came sudden and sharp, a tightening in the chest, a narrowing of breath, a spreading coldness through his limbs. He refused to be moved from his study. John sat with him in silence as Newton gazed once more into the fire.

"I have seen far," Newton whispered.

John nodded. "Yes. You have."

"Only because I stood on the shoulders of giants."

The silence stretched. The candle guttered low.

Newton's gaze softened, and for an instant he thought of the boy George, somewhere in Lincolnshire, staring at sundials, watching shadows, asking questions. A future he would never see, but which might yet carry him forward.

At last, Isaac Newton exhaled.

EPILOGUE

He was buried in Westminster Abbey, beneath a high, vaulted arch where centuries of footsteps would one day echo overhead. The living passed by in quiet waves, some hurrying through the marble aisles, others pausing. A few lingered.

Some stood still to trace the Latin inscription with their eyes, sounding out words they half understood:

Hic depositum est quod mortale fuit Isaaci Newtoni.

Here lies what was mortal of Isaac Newton.

Others came not for the words, but for the man himself, the mind that had measured the heavens and weighed the world, who had named the laws that bound planets and apples alike, who had seen invisible forces and made them speak in numbers.

He had risen from obscurity not with noise but with quiet, relentless thought. Not through war or wealth, but through questions.

And long before the cathedrals of science, before the tributes carved in stone and the museums bearing his name, there had been a boy in a barn. A small, solitary child in Woolsthorpe-by-Colsterworth, pale and serious, misunderstood and often overlooked. He was not strong. He was not loud. He was not loved for what he could do with his hands, but for what he built in his mind.

He once built a windmill from scraps, bits of wood, old nails, whatever he could find on the farm. It turned in the wind like the great sails he had seen in town. No one had taught him how.

He made water clocks and sundials, carved with care into the walls. He studied how light danced through a crack in the shutters, how shadows moved across stone. While other boys played, Isaac asked why the moon did not fall.

In the stillness of his old room at Woolsthorpe, the apple tree still stood just outside the window. Gnarled now, weathered by centuries, but standing. Its limbs stretched over the roof as they always had, casting shadows into the very spot where Newton once sat, alone with a notebook, wondering not what, but how.

Years passed. The windmill fell. The barn grew quiet. His name traveled across England, then across oceans, then beyond the bounds of Earth itself, as telescopes and satellites carried the names of Newton and his laws into the sky.

And still, somewhere in Lincolnshire, a boy named George walked through the fields near Woolsthorpe. He was nobody in particular. But as the day stretched long and the sun leaned low, he paused by a crooked tree and watched the light fall across the grass.

He did not know the name of the force that moved the sun and moon. Not yet.

But he saw the shadows shift, and he wondered.

And as long as someone wondered, Newton was not gone.

Here lies what was mortal.

But his questions still moved.

In glass, in stone, in shadow.

And in every mind brave enough to ask: "why?"